FLYING FERRETS

The Winning Team

FLYING FERGUS

The
Winning Team

CHRIS HOY
with Joanna Nadin

Illustrations by Clare Elsom

Piccadilly
PRESS

First published in Great Britain in 2017 by
Piccadilly Press
80-81 Wimpole Street, London, W1G 9RE
www.piccadillypress.co.uk

Text and illustrations copyright © Sir Chris Hoy, 2017

A CIP catalogue record for this book is available from the British Library.

ISBN: 978-1-848-12577-3
also available as an ebook

Typeset in Berkeley Oldstyle
Printed and bound by Clays Ltd, St Ives PLC

Piccadilly Press is an imprint of Bonnier Zaffre,
a Bonnier Publishing Company
www.bonnierpublishingfiction.co.uk

Meet Fergus
and his friends. . .

Chimp

Fergus

Grandpa Herc

Mum

Daisy

Jambo Patterson

Calamity Coogan

Minnie McLeod

Belinda Bruce

Wesley Wallace

Dermot Eggs

Choppy Wallace

Mikey McLeod

. . .and see where they live

Prince Waldorf

Dimmock

Knights of No Nonsense

King Woebegot

Queen Woebegot

Hounds of Horribleness

Meet Princess Lily
and her friends. . .

Princess Lily

Hector Hamilton

Unlucky Luke

Percy the Pretty Useless

The Competition

Fergus Hamilton was an ordinary nine-year-old boy. He liked biscuits (but not garibaldis, which looked like they had squashed flies in them), comics (but not really scary ones, which gave him the heebie-jeebies), and his dog Chimp (but not when he'd eaten all the biscuits – except the squashed fly ones, which not even Chimp liked). He didn't like getting up early on a Monday (but he still did it), or going to bed early on a

Sunday (but he still did it), or the way his mum made him wash behind his ears on bath nights (but he still did it in case it was true that cabbages would grow there if he didn't).

Yes, he was ordinary in almost every way, except one. Because, for a small boy, Fergus Hamilton had an extraordinarily big imagination.

Some days he imagined Chimp was a cyberdog with flashing lights and special functions like a supersonic sense of smell and x-ray vision, instead of being a rather tatty mongrel who mostly ate things he shouldn't.

Some days he imagined he lived in a flying space station, with automatic doors, beds that hovered in the air and freeze-dried meals that came out of silver packets, instead of in a flat above Grandpa's second-hand bike shop on

Napier Street, where meals mainly came from the kitchen and involved at least three vegetable portions per plate.

Some days he imagined his dad lived with them, instead of being stuck in a parallel universe called Nevermore. Fergus had been so close to rescuing him last time he visited, but as he turned the grumpy kitchen cat Suet back into his father with the help of a magic potion the dastardly King Woebegot and his Knights of No Nonsense had caught him in the act.

Next time Fergus went back, though, he and his friends Princess Lily and Unlucky Luke would outwit the King and his Knights, he was sure. And then he'd bring Dad back home and be crowned a superhero, as well as a champion cyclist.

Because right now, Fergus was imagining flying past the finishing post at the National Championships with his team, the Hercules' Hopefuls', and being crowned the fastest cyclists in all of Scotland: faster than the Southern Speedsters, faster than the Cally Cougars, faster than the Highland Hotwheels, faster even than the terrifyingly good all-girls team whose name Fergus couldn't even bring himself to think about, let alone say out loud. But most importantly, faster than their arch-rivals Wallace's

Winners, and especially their number one racer – and number one bully and bossy boots – Wesley Wallace. *I'll show him*, thought Fergus to himself as he pictured the podium and the cheering crowd. *It'll be the last time Wesley calls me a loser or a nobody. I'm not nobody. I'm somebody. I'm –*

"Fergus," interrupted Grandpa. "Earth to Fergus. Come in, Fergus."

"Huh?" Fergus blinked and saw his teammates all staring expectantly at him, and remembered with a sinking feeling where he was: not winning the Nationals in a blaze of glory, but at his kitchen table in a crunch team meeting to discuss tactics. The Nationals were still a week – and a whole lot of work – away.

"So, as I was saying," continued Grandpa, "it's not just what we do that matters, we need to know who we're up against. Wallace's Winners are definite contenders. They're clever and they're quick."

"And getting quicker," added Daisy.

"Wesley and Dermot have got their final swap down to a tee, I watched them at the track two days ago."

"And Mikey's up to something," added Minnie. "My big brother's been practicing for a flick for three weeks now."

"Nice intel," said Grandpa, nodding. "The whole team might pull that stunt so be ready for it. But we've got a bigger problem to deal with."

"Broken bikes?" asked Calamity, who was still sulking about the shenanigans at the District Championships.

Grandpa shook his head. "No, not that. We know where we stand with Choppy's lot, but there's one team we've never raced against, and never even seen in action. We know they're District Champs in their own area. We know they're all girls. We know their coach makes Champ Lamington look half-hearted."

Fergus's eyes goggled at the thought that anyone could be tougher than the man who trained his hero Steve "Spokes" Sullivan.

"They're going to have secret weapons we've never even dreamt of," Grandpa said.

"I wish we had secrets," said Daisy. "Like, what if I was actually a robot in disguise? Built specially for cycling . . ."

"Or a — a . . . monkey!" declared Calamity. "That would be cool."

"Monkeys can't cycle," said Daisy. "Then I wouldn't be a secret weapon, I'd be a setback."

"Good point," said Grandpa. "But monkeys aside, we need to discover their weak points as well as their strong ones."

Fergus thought for a moment about his secret – the one he'd been keeping for ages now: that if he cycled super fast and backpedalled three times his bike could fly to Nevermore. He wondered if that secret was a weapon or a weakness.

"Fergus, are you with us or not?" Grandpa said. "As I was saying, what I propose is a little road trip to see the opposition in training."

"Brilliant," chorused Calamity and Minnie.

"BEAST!" shouted Daisy.

"RUFF!" barked Chimp, who had woken up from his daydream about the world's biggest sausage sandwich and wanted to join in the excitement.

"Hang on, *who* are we going to see?" asked Fergus, whose own daydreaming meant he'd totally lost track. "And when?"

"Crikey, cloth ears." Grandpa grinned. "We're off first thing tomorrow morning."

"To see the speediest and scariest girls in all of Scotland," added Daisy. "Bar me, of course."

"And me!" piped up Minnie.

"You mean . . . ?"

"That's right." Grandpa nodded. "We're going to see . . . the Velociraptors."

The Velociraptors' Lair

Jambo Patterson, sports reporter on the local newspaper and Fergus's mum's fancy man, said he'd drive them. So it was in the company van, emblazoned with *Evening News* stickers, that the Hercules' Hopefuls clattered for an hour out of town before pulling to a noisy halt at the top of a hill.

"This is it, kids," Jambo announced from the driver's seat. "The home of the Velociraptors."

"Their lair!" whispered Daisy, dramatically.

"Not much of a lair," said Calamity. "Looks like a velodrome to me."

"As with everything in life, it's what's inside that counts," said Grandpa. "And that's what we're going to find out."

Fergus peered down at the sight in front of him. The track looked anything but ordinary. It was inside a walled enclosure, its smooth, sloped lanes topped by rows of polished seating. It made Middlebank look like a play park, and it made their own cinder track look like . . . well, Fergus didn't even want to think about that, it was so bad.

"How are we going to get in?" he asked instead.

"Scale the walls?" said Minnie.

"Break through the barriers!" yelled Calamity.

"Get airlifted in by invisible helicopters?" suggested Daisy, whose imagination was almost as big as Fergus's.

"Wrong, wrong and wrong again," said Grandpa. "Something far less exciting, I'm afraid." He held out six tickets. "We're going through the turnstiles with the rest of the public. It's open day."

As soon as they entered the velodrome itself, Fergus realised Grandpa had been right about something: this *was* what counted, and for the Hercules' Hopefuls it added up to one massive headache. The track was state-of-the-art, and Fergus knew the lap times the Velociraptors would be clocking up would give them a run for their money. But that was just the beginning.

"Why don't you all go and have a wander, get a feel for the place?" said Jambo.

"Aye," agreed Grandpa. "See what you can scout out. Meet back here in an hour."

"But no trying to climb through windows," called out Jambo as the foursome headed off on their fact-finding mission, Chimp at their side.

"Och." Daisy sighed. "What's a little breaking and entering between friends, eh?"

Fergus giggled. He knew she wouldn't actually try it, but the thought of acting like spies was pretty brilliant.

"What about that corridor?" asked Calamity as they passed the public toilets and rounded a corner.

"Changing rooms, it says," said Minnie. "BO-RING."

But Fergus shook his head. "Changing rooms are where the real work goes on," he said. "I read it in Spokes' autobiography. He said that's where the secret tactics are worked out."

"Then the changing rooms it is!" declared Daisy. "Only you two won't be coming, of course." She eyed Fergus and Calamity pointedly.

"Why not?" protested Fergus.

"Like, duh." Daisy rolled her eyes. "Girls only."

"Fine by me," said Fergus. "We'll take the training ground. Coming, Calamity?"

But Calamity was already heading off towards what looked like the cafeteria.

Fergus sighed. "That boy could sniff out a hot dog from a hundred miles."

At the words "hot dog", Chimp looked up from the railing he'd been licking. Fergus rubbed the top of his head. "Looks like it's just you and me, boy. Ready for some sleuthing?" Fergus knew Chimp was probably more ready for a hot dog, but he knew his dog was faithful, too. And so, side-by-side, the pair set off on the search for secrets.

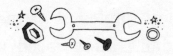

"Training area," declared the sign in bold, black letters. "No entry."

"I'll pretend I didn't see it," said Fergus. "Besides, who's going to spot us, eh, Chimp? Everyone's out at the track watching the demo race." And with that reassuring thought, he pushed at the door.

Fergus gasped at the sight that awaited him. Behind the door wasn't so much a training area but a torture chamber.

Twelve high-tech exercise bikes stood in three rows of four in the centre of the room, then around the edges were all manner of complicated looking machines Fergus recognized from his magazines. Some were to strengthen your legs, some to build up your arms, and some that looked like the stretching racks he'd learned about in history at school.

Fergus read from the typed and laminated sign on the wall:

THE RULES

**4 hours of exercise to be completed
EACH and EVERY day,
including:**

**50 lunges
75 squats
100 push-ups
and 1 full inch-adder**

**No TV
No Video Games
No Shenanigans, Tomfoolery
or Malarkey of any kind.**

"No fun, more like," Fergus whispered to Chimp. And what was an inch-adder anyway, he wondered, eyeing the rack.

Maybe they really were stretching the

girls out to lengthen them! "But making their legs longer would be cheating!" he said.

"Ruff!" agreed Chimp.

"Wrong," said another voice.

Fergus whipped round to find himself face to face with the most terrifying woman he had ever seen. Her hair was the same steely grey as her tracksuit, and her forehead was a permanent frown.

"Are . . . are you . . . ?" stammered Fergus.

THE RULES
4 hours of exercise to be completed EACH and EVERY day, including:

50 lunges
75 squats
100 push-ups
and 1 full inch-adder

No TV
No Video Games
No Shenanigans, Tomfoolery or Malarkey of any kind.

"Major Margaret Menzies?" said the woman. "Yes. And you are? No, don't bother – all you are is an ignorant sneak. If you knew anything you'd know that, to be the best team, following strict diets and exercise regimes are common sense, and being super-stretched is entirely within the rules."

"But it's unfair –" interrupted Fergus.

Major Menzies held up her hand to shush him, so he shushed. "And you'd *also* know that this area is strictly out of bounds. Now come with me, boy." She grabbed Fergus by the collar.

"Ow!" he yelled.

It was Chimp's turn to protest, barking angrily at the woman, who in turn eyed the mutt with disgust.

"And bring that germ-bucket with you."

Without a single further utterance,

she marched Fergus and Chimp out of the room, down the corridor and back to the turnstiles where Grandpa was waiting.

"Well, well, well," said Major Menzies, eyeing the old man with disdain. "If it isn't Hercules Hamilton. I might have known this . . . this *ruffian* had something to do with you."

"Maggie." Grandpa nodded.

"You know her?" Fergus gasped.

"Old army friends." Grandpa smiled at Fergus.

"Enemies, more like," snapped Major Menzies.

"Rivals, maybe," conceded Grandpa. "Still are."

"Hercules' Hopefuls is your team?"

Grandpa smiled. "Yup. Which you'd know if you'd done your homework, of course. Just like we're doing ours. And I reckon we've got all we need to know, so I'll see you in a week, hey, Maggie? We'll give you a wave from the winners' podium."

"In your dreams," scowled Major Menzies. "It'll be us up there and you know it."

"Fifty pounds says you're wrong," said Grandpa.

Fergus felt his tummy go funny. Grandpa didn't bet on things. And what if they lost? How would Grandpa find fifty pounds to pay Major Menzies? All their spare money had gone on setting up the training track and the new team kit.

"Done," said the woman.

"But . . ." Fergus began.

"But nothing," said Major Menzies.

Then, to Fergus's horror, the pair spat on their hands and shook them. "Gross," he said.

"Old army tradition," said Grandpa, as Major Menzies stalked off, wiping her hand on her jacket. "Now come on, let's find the others and head home. We've got some work to do."

"I thought you said we'd finished our homework?"

"Finished?" Grandpa laughed. "We've only just begun."

A New Regime

Grandpa hadn't been joking. The next few days Fergus worked harder than he'd ever worked in his life. Daisy and Minnie had found out from the changing rooms that the Velociraptors trained in two layers of clothing to make them hotter so it was harder work, and Calamity hadn't just found food in the cafeteria after all, but a special diet plan that included liver on a daily basis for extra iron. Grandpa had decided that the only way to beat the girls was to join them, with more training, in more clothes, and without any sweets and treats – including marmalade sandwiches.

"Och, I'm sweating like a racehorse in here," Fergus moaned, pulling at the neck of the woolly jumper he was wearing on top of his racing jersey. "And I'm starving."

"Piffle and poppycock," said Grandpa. "You're just getting used to it, that's all. Besides, it'll be worth it when you take the jumper off before the race and we win that trophy."

"You mean when you win that fifty pounds," muttered Fergus.

"I heard that," snapped Grandpa grouchily. Then he said in a softer voice, "Okay, it'd be nice to win the bet, but not for the money, just to prove to that old show-off that I'm not the lily-livered loser she thinks I am."

Daisy groaned. "Don't mention liver again, please," she begged.

"Did she really call you a loser?" Fergus asked.

"Aye." Grandpa nodded. "And more besides, back in our army days."

"Then we'll show her," said Fergus. "We'll use all our secret weapons and prove that we don't need stretching to win anything."

"What secret weapons have we got?" asked Minnie, scratching at her own sweaty outfit. "We haven't got any weapons. Or even secrets. The other teams know everything about us already."

"I can touch my nose with the tip of my tongue," said Daisy, proving it.

"I've broken my leg twice," said Calamity, proudly. "And dislocated my shoulder seventeen times."

"Well, that's not something we want to let on," said Grandpa. "And Minnie would you stop wiggling and jiggling. You're giving me the heebie-jeebies just watching you."

"I can't help it," moaned Minnie. "It's all these clothes. They're making me itch."

Fergus sighed and thought about Nevermore again. He badly wanted to tell his friends what he could do. But they'd never believe him. Sometimes he hardly believed it himself. Only maybe . . . "I've got a secret," he started to say. "Sometimes I –"

"Hang on a minute," interrupted Grandpa. "Minnie, what's that spot on your neck?"

"What spot?" she asked.

"*Which* spot, more like," said Daisy. "You're covered in them, look."

Minnie looked.

So did Fergus, and gasped. Daisy was right. Minnie was covered from head to toe in red, angry-looking spots.

"The plague!" yelled Daisy, moving away.

"Fleas!" cried Calamity. "From Chimp!"

"Hey!" protested Fergus crossly. "Chimp's as clean as a whistle." He looked down at the dog, who was rolling in a muddy puddle. "Well, maybe not that clean," he admitted. "But he doesn't have fleas. Perhaps they're your fleas!" He looked angrily at Calamity.

"Hey, hey," Grandpa said. "No one has fleas. But I think someone very definitely has a case of the old chicken pox."

Minnie gulped. "Oh no! Suki Chan got them off her cousin – she's been off sick since Friday. But on Thursday I was sitting next to her in class."

"Bingo," said Grandpa. "Or rather, blimey. That's put a blooming big spanner in the works."

"Why?" asked Fergus. "It's only spots."

Grandpa shook his head. "It's not only spots. You can start feeling worn out or get quite poorly. Besides, chicken pox

30

is contagious. Minnie will be banned from meets for a month."

Fergus felt his heart sink. "Now what?" he asked. "The Nationals are just days away and we can't race with only three of us."

"I can do tricks to distract them," said Calamity, trying to pull his bike round in a rock walk. "Then they'll never notice that – WOOOAH!" he yelled as he flipped backwards, the bike landing on top of him in an awkward heap.

"Are you okay?" gasped Fergus, sinking to the ground.

"I– I– ow!" stammered Calamity as Fergus tried to extricate his friend from the spokes. "That really, really hurts!"

Fergus peered hard at Calamity's hand. "Er, Grandpa?" asked Fergus. "Are wrists supposed to bend that far back?"

"Noooooo!" wailed Calamity.

"No," agreed Grandpa. "That looks like it's –"

"Broken," Calamity finished. Then added, "Again."

"I'll be able to ride again, won't I?" sobbed Calamity, as the ambulance arrived.

"Aye," assured Grandpa.

"By Saturday?" asked Calamity hopefully.

"Aye, by Saturday," laughed a voice behind them. "Saturday next season!"

Fergus spun round to see the smirking face of Wesley Wallace and his sidekick, Dermot Eggs.

"Next season," repeated Dermot.

"Next year!" Wesley laughed.

"That's enough," Grandpa snapped. "Go and do something useful, why don't you?"

"Like get trapped in a dungeon," murmured Fergus.

"Is Wesley right?" asked Calamity,

after the pair had stomped off to look for other people to pester.

Grandpa lowered his head. "I'm sorry, sonny," he said to Calamity, as the ambulance doors shut. "But you're out of the race too."

"It's hopeless," Fergus moaned, as he and Grandpa and Chimp trudged up the stairs to the flat. "We've no chance now of even competing, let alone beating Wallace's Winners."

"Or the Velociraptors," added Grandpa sadly, opening the front door.

"Whatever." Fergus flopped down at the kitchen table with a sigh.

"Hey, what's with the long face?"

Fergus raised his head enough to see Jambo holding a ladder and Mum at the top of it painting the ceiling.

Jambo was always round these days, and at first Fergus thought he'd mind. But actually, he had to admit, it was pretty ace. Jambo was great at helping out around the house, plus he loved to watch football on TV, especially when Hearts were playing, and he hated broccoli as much as Fergus so now Mum only did peas.

But not even Jambo could fix this.

"Has the world ended?" Jambo asked.

"Might as well have." Fergus sighed and let his head drop onto the table with a clunk.

"Two of the team are out." Grandpa sat down as heavy-hearted as Fergus. "Calamity's broken his arm and Minnie's got the pox."

Jambo thought for a moment. "Well, if Minnie's got the pox, that means Mikey probably will have too."

"Aye," agreed Mum. "And I heard from Mrs MacCafferty that Belinda Bruce ate four boxes of Bruce's Big Ones toffee-chocolate crunches in one go, and now she's got a dicky tummy and is banned from training by the doctor."

"Is that supposed to cheer me up?" asked Fergus.

"No," admitted Mum, "just that you're not the only ones with problems."

"All that means is both teams are out

of the race." Grandpa sighed. "They might as well just hand the trophy to the Velociraptors right now."

"Unless . . . " began Jambo.

"Unless what?" asked Fergus and Grandpa together.

"A word, Herc," said Jambo and beckoned him over before whispering quietly.

"It could work," said Grandpa.

"What could work?" demanded Fergus. "Tell me!"

"All in good time," said Grandpa. "All in good time."

"He's right," said Mum. "You just concentrate on staying fit. That means eating your liver and onions, then getting a decent night's sleep."

Fergus's stomach swirled at the thought of another plateful of gloopy sauce and gristly meat, but his heart lifted. Jambo and Grandpa had a plan. He didn't yet know what it was, but if the smiles on their faces were anything to go by, their plan was a winner.

Just like he would be.

Keep Your Enemies Close

Fergus stared up at the Wallace's Wheels sign above the window.

"I don't get it," he said. "Some big plan. We've walked down the road and now we're at Choppy's shop."

"All will become clear," said Grandpa, mysteriously, pushing the door open so that an electronic beep sounded noisily. "Any minute now."

Fergus followed Grandpa inside, still wondering what on earth they were up to. Choppy Wallace and Wesley looked up from pricing up a new batch of Sullivan Swifts.

"What do you want, Hamilton?" asked Choppy grumpily.

"Come to concede the race now you're two team members down?" gloated Wesley.

"Hardly," said Grandpa. "From what I hear, you boys are in as sticky a situation as we are."

Choppy slammed the sticker gun down on the counter. "And where'd you hear that?" he demanded.

"A little bird told me," said Grandpa.

"More like an enormous Mrs MacCafferty," sneered Choppy. "I might have known she'd blab."

"Och, does it matter?" asked Grandpa. "The point is the race is tomorrow, we're both in trouble, and if we don't put our heads together, literally, both our teams will be out of the Nationals."

"What do you mean 'put our heads together'?" asked Choppy.

"Yeah, what *do* you mean?" asked Fergus slowly, a worrying picture forming in his head.

"Exactly that," said Grandpa. "We join forces. You've got two riders left, so have we. So we put two and two together and we've got a team. And not just any team but . . ."

" . . . the fastest team in the country," finished Choppy, gazing into the distance at the idea.

Fergus felt his stomach sink into his shoes. "Are you mad?" he asked.

"Crazy?" added Wesley.

"Loop the loop?" Fergus cried.

"Doo-flipping-lally?" Wesley wailed.

"Well, you boys agree on something."
Grandpa laughed. "That's a start."

"We don't agree on *anything*," retorted
Wesley. "Do we, Hamilton?"

Fergus shook his head. "No, we jolly
well don't!"

Grandpa shrugged. "Well, it's team
up or no one gets to race at all."

Fergus swallowed his first thought, which was "So what?" when he realized the truth of what Grandpa had said. Here was a chance to compete, and not only that – a chance to win. He and Wesley were the fastest individual riders on record. And Daisy and Dermot weren't far behind. Together they might just have a chance of snatching victory from the jaws of the Velociraptors.

He nodded slowly. "Okay," he said.

Wesley, who wasn't as stupid as he looked, had come to the same conclusion. "Fine," he spat. "But on one condition."

"What's that?" asked Grandpa.

"I get to wear Number One."

Fergus felt his fists clench in anger. He'd worked hard for that jersey and he wasn't going to give it up just like that, especially not to Wesley Wallace.

"No way!" Fergus protested. "I'd rather forfeit."

"You wouldn't!" snapped Wesley.

"Would so!" exclaimed Fergus.

"Wouldn't!" repeated Wesley.

"That's enough, boys," said Grandpa, holding up his hands.

"Agreed," said Choppy. "It doesn't matter who wears the jersey."

"Then you won't care if I do," said Fergus.

Wesley looked furious. "But I'm faster. I'm down to two minutes four seconds a lap."

"Fergie?" asked Grandpa.

Fergus felt his stomach sink. "Two minutes eight," he said.

"Then that decides it," said Choppy.

Fergus looked at Grandpa for help, but Grandpa shrugged. "Let him wear it, sonny. You can be Number Two and

Daisy and Dermot can toss a coin for the others."

Choppy nodded in agreement. "Sounds fair to me."

"And me." Wesley grinned.

"Fine," said Fergus, knowing he was beaten three to one. But it wasn't fine. And he was going to do something about it.

"Come on, Chimp," he said as soon as they were outside, leaving Grandpa to sort out the small print. "I know how we can fix this." And with that he sprinted home to fetch his bike, Chimp bounding happily after him.

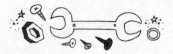

Fergus checked over his shoulder to make sure no one was hanging around, scouting him out for secrets. Satisfied that everyone on Carnoustie Common was going about their own business rather than minding his, Fergus tightened the strap on his helmet, and pushed down hard on his pedals. "I'll prove who's best," he said to himself as he flew across the cinders. "I'll get my dad back here. Wesley might be faster than me, but he can't fly on his bike, can he? Ready, Chimp?"

Chimp barked his reply.

"Then brace yourself for a bump," Fergus yelled as he closed his eyes and let the pedals slip backwards. "Three, two, one . . ."

The Dungeon of Despair

Fergus looked around at the grey stone walls and the bars across the small, high-up window.

"Oops," he said.

"Oops?" demanded Chimp in his now-familiar Aussie accent. "We're stuck in the slammer and all you can say is 'oops'?"

"I was thinking about Dad and the Dungeon of Despair," apologised Fergus.

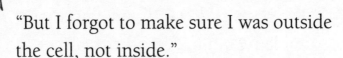

"But I forgot to make sure I was outside the cell, not inside."

"Fergus?" came another familiar voice. "Is that you?"

"Lily?" Fergus called into the gloom, then grinned broadly as the face of his friend appeared in a hatch in the heavy wooden door. "What are you doing here?"

"I've been waiting for you!" she cried. "And never mind me, what are *you* doing in *there*?"

"I've been asking the same question," grumbled Chimp. "Of all the places in all of Nevermore and he gets us banged up before we've even committed a crime."

"Oh, I wouldn't say that," came a friendly voice from what seemed like the cell next door. "Just being in Nevermore without a permit is enough to get you sent down for a hundred years."

Fergus felt a flicker of electricity spark through him. "Dad?" he asked hopefully.

"Aye," replied Hector, "it's me, all right. They brought me down here a few hours ago after you left."

"Then we're in time!" exclaimed Fergus.

"To do what?" asked Lily.

Fergus stared at her as if she'd lost her mind. "Er, to get Dad out of here. Then I can take him back home in time for the Nationals?"

"Now, hang on . . . " said Hector.

"The thing is . . . " added Lily.

Fergus was confused. "What could be more important?"

Lily looked at him hard and seemed to shake herself for a second, before smiling again, to Fergus's relief. "No, you're right," she said. "We need to get you both out of here."

"But –" began Hector.

"No buts!" Fergus interrupted.

"He's right, mate," added Chimp. "Butts are for sitting on." Then he turned to Fergus. "So what's the plan, Stan?"

Fergus shrugged. "Well, I hadn't quite got that far yet."

Lily rolled her eyes. "Easy-peasy. We just make some noise. A LOT of noise."

"And then what?" asked Fergus.

Lily smiled. "Oh, you'll see."

And so between the four of them shouting and stamping and singing a song Chimp knew about a kangaroo they kicked up a racket loud enough to send the rats scuttling for their holes, and the keys on the prison guard's chain rattling against his enormous thigh, which in turn sent him thudding slowly and heavily to find out what was going on down in the dungeon.

Fergus gulped as a huge angry face scowled through the hatch.

"Ah, Lunk," Lily greeted the stranger in the passageway. "So glad you could join us."

"What's that boy doin' in there?" demanded the thug. "'oo is he, anyway? And what's 'e got a monkey for?"

"Oi!" protested Chimp. "I'm a pure-bred mongrel dog, I'll have you know."

Lunk snorted. "Could've fooled me."

"Anyone could fool you," said Lily.

"What?" Lunk demanded.

"Oh, nothing," Lily said, airily. "Now the thing is, this boy and that man in there have insulted me and the king several times."

"Er, no we haven't," said Fergus, confused.

Lily shot him a look before turning back to Lunk. "And now he's lying. And you know what the penalty for lying to royalty is, don't you?"

Lunk nodded, and let out a nasty laugh. "Death!" he said with a satisfied smile.

"But – " began Fergus.

"Butts are for sitting on," repeated Lily. "And I'll thank you to keep quiet.

Now, Lunk, death can come later, but right now I think my father King Woebegot would be very pleased with you if you released them and marched them straight to his chamber for trial, don't you?"

Lunk thought, and then thought some more, and then slowly began to nod his gigantic head.

"King," he said. "To the king."

So that was how Fergus found himself being dragged off by the collar for the second time in as many days. Only this time his dad was being dragged beside him, while Chimp was trapped under one of Lunk's armpits.

"And it don't smell too sweet, I can tell you," moaned the dog.

"Nearly there," said Lily, walking alongside them. "And then . . . death."

Fergus shuddered. He still didn't understand what, exactly, Lily was up to. But the princess was his friend, and he had to believe she knew what she was doing.

Didn't she?

Fergus didn't have time to ponder.

Two enormous doors swung open to reveal a vast chamber decorated entirely in gold, and at the far end sat two thin and rather cross-looking people in crowns: King and Queen Woebegot. Lily hurried towards them.

"Ah, there you are, Elisabeth-Jane," snapped the woman in a voice like cut crystal. "How many times have I told you not to go wandering orf like that? It's not in the least princess-like."

"It's Lily, how many times have I told you? And Wesley does it," said Lily sulkily.

"Yes, well, he's – "

"– a boy?" interrupted Lily.

"A bozo, more like," said Chimp.

Fergus clamped a hand over his mutt's mouth, but it was too late.

"Who said that?" snapped King Woebegot.

"Er, I did," Fergus piped up quickly.

"No, he didn't," insisted Chimp. "It was me!"

"A talking monkey!" screeched the queen. "That's against the law. Orf with its head!"

"How many times?" muttered Chimp. "I mean, do I look like I have opposable thumbs or a prehensile tail?"

"Well you do look awfully grubby," said the queen. "Which is against the law. Orf with your head, I say!"

"No one's head's coming orf – I mean off," said Lily quickly. "This is Fergus and his DOG Chimp and they're here because they want to take Hector home."

"Who's Hector?" demanded the king.

"That would be me," Fergus's dad spoke.

"Oh, you!" bellowed the king in a surprisingly loud voice for such a skinny man. "I thought I'd put you back behind bars. I might have known you'd try to escape. You – you bike brute! You cycling schemer!"

"But, Daddy," said Lily. "Isn't this the best plan? If Fergus and Chimp take Hector back to Scotland then you won't have all of them taking up valuable space in the dungeon, will you?"

Fergus crossed his fingers, and his toes, and even his legs as the king fell into deep thought.

"Clever," he said eventually. "We'll make a princess of you yet. I've thought about it and the answer is . . . absolutely not and orf with their heads."

Fergus's legs weakened and began to wobble, but then to his surprise he felt the arm of his dad holding him steady. "I'm right here," whispered Hector. "I'll protect you."

Part of Fergus wanted to shout at his dad then, to tell him that if he'd thought about that earlier – if he'd never disappeared off to Nevermore in the first place – then they wouldn't be in this mess, they'd all be safe at home on Napier Street with Mum and Grandpa, all together. But the touch of his father's hand was overwhelming, and in that instant, Fergus forgave him everything and let himself sink into his dad's arms.

"You can't chop off their heads!" protested Lily.

"Er, he can," said Lunk.

"But –" Lily interjected.

Before Chimp could point out again what butts were for, a small, squat man wearing a cloak and a worried look ran hurriedly through a side door. "Your majesties!" he panted. "It's Waldorf."

King Woebegot sighed heavily. "What has that . . . boy done now?" he demanded.

"It's his Hover 3000," gabbled the messenger. "Him and that Dimwit –"

"Dimmock!" interrupted the queen.

"Sorry, your majesty, Dimmock, your majesty," corrected the messenger. "Him and Dimmock have run out of petrol."

"So tell them to walk home," said the king. "That will teach him to disobey orders. He knows there's a fuel shortage."

"That's the thing," said the messenger. "They can't. Because the Hover 3000 is sort of . . . stuck."

"Stuck where, exactly?" asked the queen.

"In the middle of the swamp," said the messenger. "The Swamp . . . of Certain Death."

Queen Woebegot gasped and fainted. King Woebegot dropped his enormous and pointless orb. "Send for the Knights

of No Nonsense," he called.

"Can't, sir," said the messenger. "They're out of fuel, too."

"The horses need fuel?" whispered Chimp.

"Hover bikes!" hissed Lily. "This isn't the Dark Ages, you know."

"Our precious Waldorf is doomed!" wailed the queen who had woken up, and then promptly fainted again.

But he's not, thought Fergus. *Not if . . .*

"I'll go!" he piped up.

"What?" asked the king.

"What?" echoed Chimp.

"I'll go," repeated Fergus. "With Lily. On our bikes. They don't need petrol so we can get to the swamp in seconds."

"He's right," Lily nodded furiously. "The bikes are Waldorf's only hope."

"If you're going, then I'm going with you," declared Hector.

Fergus's heart jumped. "Really?"

"Really!" said his dad. "This is dangerous stuff. You need me at your side." And he stepped forward to stand by Fergus. But Lunk grabbed Hector's collar again and yanked him up and back, so he dangled uselessly.

"I don't think so," said the king.

"But..." spluttered Hector, "my son needs me. What if Fergus gets sucked into the swamp himself?"

"Then I won't have to chop his head off later along with yours," said the King. "He can go with Lily, but you stay here."

Fergus felt his legs shake again, but his dad squeezed his arm. "I'm sorry, son," he said. "I tried. But you can do it, Fergus," he added. "I know you can. You're a Hamilton through and through."

And Fergus knew he could, or at least he could give it a jolly good try. "I'll be back as soon as I can," said Fergus to his dad, and grabbed a relieved Chimp from Lunk's sweaty armpit.

"Wait for me!" yelled Lily as Fergus began to head for the door.

"Where do you think you're going, young lady?" demanded the queen who had woken up again.

"To save my brother!" Lily answered. "Not that he deserves it."

And with the thud of the queen fainting for a third time behind them, Fergus, Chimp and Lily fled down the passageway to fetch the bikes.

The Swamp of Certain Death

Fergus hadn't been lying. Having zoomed past the Well of Everlasting Torment, and whizzed through the Gruesome Glade, avoiding a slippery serpent or two, they were at the Swamp of Certain Death in what seemed like seconds. Waldorf and Dimmock were sitting on top of the Hover 3000, which was slowly but surely sinking into the sticky mud.

"Lily!" cried Waldorf, smiling at the

sight of his sister for possibly the first time ever. "Oh." His face fell as he clocked Fergus. "And *you*. What do you want?"

"Oh, only to save you," said Fergus. "But if you'd rather get sucked into oblivion, then be my guest."

"No, no," said Waldorf, hurriedly. "Saving would be . . . excellent. But how?"

"Like this!" Cycling forward, Lily leaned over her back wheel and pulled hard on the handlebars so the front wheel lifted off the ground. Then she bounced up and down on the back wheel like an excited rabbit.

"What's that?" asked Waldorf.

"A bunny hop!" Fergus replied. "Nice one, Lily."

"I just need to get some more height," she said, bouncing for all she was worth.

"It's no use," Fergus said. "I mean, that's brilliotic, but you'll still end up in the mud as soon as you try to go near the hovermobile."

"Oh, great," said Waldorf. "I knew it. You and your useless bikes."

"Hey," said Fergus. "If it wasn't for these bikes getting here in record time you'd be doomed anyway."

"Hang on," said Lily. "Riding's so

beast on its own that I forgot about this." She pushed a button on the bike's control panel, did another bunny hop and it immediately jumped high above the ground. "Emergency Jet Boost. I've also got smoke, lemonade, and a flap that dispenses moist towellettes."

The magic buttons! Fergus had forgotten about those from his first visit. Of course! He found the jet boost button on his own bike and pushed it, feeling himself shoot up beside Lily in an enormous bunny hop.

"We just need to time it right and we can grab them as we go past," Fergus said, as they landed again.

"Grab on as we go past!" Chimp called to Waldorf, as Fergus prepared to jump.

"You too," Lily said to Dimmock. "I suppose."

Together Lily and Fergus bunny-hopped with extra jet boost, then pedalled fast through the air straight to the centre of the swamp.

Fergus felt the bike begin to sink as Waldorf grabbed the bike frame.

"Just in time," declared Lily as they landed.

They all watched as the top of the Hover 3000 sank beneath the surface of the swamp with an enormous "glup".

"To the castle!" called Lily.

"To the castle," agreed Fergus, slightly less excitedly, given what was waiting for him there. But it was time, he told himself. So with Waldorf's arms tight around him, he headed back to the castle to face his fate.

"That was . . . outstanding!" cried Waldorf, as he hopped off at the door to the royal chamber.

"What, being rescued by your sister?" asked Fergus, teasing.

"Oh, ha ha," said Waldorf. "No, riding the bike! It was so much more fun than the hovermobile. I want a bike!"

"Told you so," said Lily, forcibly removing Dimmock, who had been clutching at her, eyes tight shut.

"You were right all along," said Waldorf. "Bicycles shouldn't be banned. They should be . . ."

"Celebrated?" suggested Fergus.

"Raced?" added Chimp, cheekily.

"Raced . . . that's it!" agreed Waldorf. "We should set up a bike race. I'm going to tell Father right this minute."

Fergus grinned as he felt something inside him soar at the possibility. Could it really happen here, in Nevermore? Cycling restored to the status of a national sport?

"Over my dead body!" announced King Woebegot. "Though welcome back, Waldorf, and I'll punish you later."

"But if I had a bicycle I wouldn't need

punishing," replied his son. "Because I'd never be tempted to steal the hovermobiles and get into trouble."

Fergus shook his head in disbelief. All this time he'd written off Waldorf as a fool but he was way smarter than he looked.

"He's right," Fergus said, nodding at the prince. "Bikes are good for you."

"They give you focus," added Hector, who was still dangling from Lunk's fat hand. "Keep you fit and healthy."

"But they're dangerous!" wailed the queen.

"Not if you wear the right clothes," said Lily. "And learn to ride them properly."

"And besides," said Fergus. "It's the hovermobiles that turned out to be dangerous. The bikes were super safe!"

The queen's lips tightened – a look Fergus recognized from Mrs D, Daisy's mum. But Mrs D had been won over in the end. So maybe . . .

"What if I took charge?" suggested Hector. "Made sure they rode safely."

King Woebegot looked thoughtful, but Fergus felt his stomach lurch. "How can you?" he asked, turning to his dad. "You're coming home with me."

"Besides," said Queen Woebegot, "he's still a criminal. Orf with his head!"

Hector turned to his son, or tried to, though it was quite hard with Lunk's tight grip on him. "Fergie, I *am* home. That's what I wanted to tell you earlier."

Fergus gave Lily an angry look. "This was your idea, wasn't it? That's why you were in the prison earlier, persuading him."

"No!" she insisted.

"It's the truth," added Hector. "It was my decision."

"But . . . " began Fergus.

"You know what butts are for," said

his dad softly. "Besides, you've done fine without me for years. Better than fine, in fact. Big race tomorrow, isn't it?"

Fergus felt a jolt as he remembered. "I . . ."

"So go," insisted Hector.

The hard seed of an idea began to unfurl softly inside Fergus. "Then after the Nationals I could come back," he said. "Be a part of it here."

"Hang on a minute there, matey," piped up Chimp. "We don't even know if there's an 'it' to be part of."

Fergus, Lily, Waldorf and Hector all turned expectantly to the king.

"Oh . . . very well," King Woebegot said at last. "Cycling is officially reinstated. And Hector, I officially pardon you for beating me on your bicycle. But if anything happens to my children, then it really will be off with your head."

Hector smiled. "I'll watch them," he said. "Don't you worry."

"And there will be rules," the king insisted. "Mark my words."

"A lot of them," snapped the queen.

"Fergus," continued the king, "I have something for you. A little thank you." And he whispered to Lunk who disappeared out of the door, only to return a minute later with a large glass jar containing . . .

"My bell!" exclaimed Hector. "From the original Hamilton Herc! You kept it all this time."

"Indeed," said the king. "Now, if I may, I'd like to give this to Fergus, for his own bike."

"Be my guest," said Hector. "I'd be honoured."

King Woebegot took the lid off the jar and handed the bell to Fergus. "Here you are," he said. "I'll expect to see it in full use in training. Can't have any accidents, can we?"

"No, your majesty," said Fergus, feeling the weight of it in his hand, and giving it a ding for good measure.

"Don't I get a bell?" demanded Waldorf.

"Of course," sighed the king. "And a helmet. And a jersey."

"I'll get to wear Number One, of course," said Waldorf.

"Will not!" retorted Lily.

"Will too!" insisted Waldorf.

"Hey, hey," interrupted Hector. "Who cares who gets to wear what? You both get to ride. Isn't that the most important thing?"

Fergus smiled as the green shoots of possibility grew into real promise. He'd get to ride *here*, in Nevermore, and spend time with his dad – he could stay for longer.

Forever, perhaps.

But first, he had some goodbyes to say back home. And one last race to win on Scottish soil.

Number One

"'Hercules' Hopefuls'?" asked Wesley, looking grimly at his new team jersey. "What was wrong with Wallace's Winners?"

"About a *bazillion* things," muttered Fergus.

"Look, we had to pick one team name in order to qualify," said Grandpa. "And the only fair way seemed to be to toss a coin."

Choppy didn't look too thrilled about it either. But for once he agreed with Grandpa. "It's just for one race, Wesley," he said, "then you'll be back on Wallace's Winners again."

"Besides," Grandpa added, "haven't we got bigger things to worry about?" He nodded over to where the Velociraptors were warming up under the military command of Major Menzies.

They'd already done fifty push-ups each and were now on some complicated squat-thrust combinations.

"Suppose," said Wesley, turning back and eyeing Fergus. "At least I've got the right number on my jersey," he boasted. "And I don't have a baby BELL on my handlebars."

"It's not a BABY bell," protested Fergus.

"It might weigh you down, though," Daisy pointed out.

"Get in the way, more like," said Wesley.

"Where did you get it anyway?" asked Grandpa, looking at it curiously. "It looks familiar – did it come from my shop?"

Fergus smiled. "A friend gave it to me," he replied. "For luck. And I'm keeping it."

Wesley rolled his eyes. "Weirdo," he said and wheeled himself straight off to the starting line in an enormous huff.

"Listen." Grandpa pulled Daisy and Fergus into their usual team huddle. "This isn't going to be easy," he warned them. "You're not used to working with Wesley and Dermot. But you've got a real chance to show those dinosaurs what you're made of."

Fergus grinned. "And show Major Menzies what *you're* made of, Grandpa."

"And win you that fifty quid!" exclaimed Daisy.

"Aye, well, that would be a nice bonus, it's true," admitted Grandpa. "But money's neither here nor there when it comes to pride."

"We'll do our best," promised Fergus. "Won't we, Dais?"

Daisy nodded. "Anything for you, coach."

Grandpa smiled. "And for Minnie and Calamity, too. The team's bigger than us three, don't forget it."

"And Mum," added Fergus, "she's part of the team as well."

"Aye." Grandpa nodded. "She certainly is."

"So's Jambo," Daisy pointed out.

Fergus looked over to where his mum and her boyfriend were standing in the crowd, both wearing the Hercules' Hopefuls team colours and holding a homemade banner that read "Flying Fergus and Daredevil Daisy". He rolled his eyes, but smiled at the same time. "You're right," he said. Jambo had done loads for the team, and for him and his mum too. He'd never seen Mum this happy. Not even the time she won a year's supply of dog shampoo at the bingo. Which reminded him . . .

"And Chimp," he said. "Chimp's our mascot, after all."

Grandpa laughed and gave Fergus a squeeze. "Do it for all of us, eh? This team's one big, happy family. And today, we've got two extra members."

"Yeah, the Ugly Stepbrothers," said Daisy.

Fergus glanced over to Wesley and Dermot who were already bent low over their handlebars, bracing themselves for the race ahead. It was going to be hard to think of them as family. But this was his last chance to prove himself to everyone here; his last race as a Hercules' Hopeful. What was it that his favourite film superspy Johnnie Wiseman was always saying? That was it: "Keep your friends close, but keep your enemies closer." And with that, Fergus felt determination rise up in him, fiery and strong.

"Let's do it," he announced. "Let's win this thing."

The Nationals

"On your marks!" called the umpire.

Fergus looked to his left and nodded at Daisy, then to his right where Wesley and Dermot were lined up. "We can do this," he whispered.

Wesley glanced back at him, for once his face reflecting Fergus's own feelings. "We can," he insisted. "We really can."

"Get set!" the umpire warned them.

Both boys turned back to face the front, their feet poised on the pedals, their hands tightly gripping the handlebars.

This is it, thought Fergus. Any second now the biggest race of his cycling career was going to begin. And if he was going to bow out, he was jolly well going to do his damnedest to do it as National Champion. He took a deep breath.

"GO!"

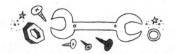

The Hopefuls were off to a flying start, overtaking the Cally Cougars and Southern Speedsters within what felt like seconds. That left the Highland Hotwheels in second place, and in first place the Velociraptors, led by terrifying twins Lulu and Lala Jones.

Fergus pushed down harder and harder, helped along by his position, snug in Daisy's slipstream.

"Nice one, Fergie!" he heard Calamity shout from the stands.

"You can do it, Dais," yelled Minnie, who was right by his side, pale as a ghost from the calamine lotion.

Fergus felt Daisy shift up, giving it that little bit more to power past the Speedsters. He followed suit, digging down deep to find some extra energy, assuming Dermot and Wesley were doing the same alongside them. But then he heard it.

"Pull back, Wesley!"

It was Grandpa. Fergus glanced to check what the boys were up to and saw to his horror that Wesley wasn't in his position behind Dermot but was pushing out into the front of the team, determined, no doubt, to live up to the number on his jersey.

"Not yet!" Fergus yelled at him. "Save some energy."

"Fat chance," Wesley yelled back. "No way you're taking this from me, Hamilton!"

"Pull back, Wesley!"

Not even Choppy's screaming could stop him. Wesley wasn't letting anyone take number one position from him, not even his own team members, and especially not Fergus. Wesley nudged forwards, forcing Daisy to lead Dermot while he formed a barrier in front of Fergus. *Wesley thinks I'm the enemy,* Fergus thought to himself. *Not the Velociraptors – me!*

Okay, Fergus decided. I've got two choices: let him hold us all back because he's too tired but still won't let me through. Or bide my time, and hope for a miracle.

I'll take the miracle, he thought. *I'm not giving up.*

The teams rounded the far bend, heading back up the home straight. There were just centimetres separating them now. Time was running out.

Then Lulu Jones lost control for just a second and went wide, sending their third rider into a panic as she automatically did the same. Daisy saw her chance and slipped inside, Wesley mirroring her only moments later.

"Lucky!" he said.

"No, clever," she hissed back.

There were only two Velociraptors ahead of them now. If Daisy *and* Wesley pulled back Fergus could romp home with Dermot, he just knew it. But not even Daisy was budging.

"What are you doing?" he yelled. "It's time."

"Trust me!" Daisy yelled back.

Fergus did trust her. With his life, if necessary. But this wasn't what they'd planned and worked so hard at. He hoped really hard she knew what she was doing.

Down the slick concrete they spun, their wheels a blur as they passed stand after stand of cheering fans. *This is how Spokes must have felt*, thought Fergus, remembering that it was this very race that put Spokes in the spotlight and started his international career.

But Spokes had won. And unless that miracle happened soon, Fergus was going to lose out to Lala Jones who had just pulled ahead of her Velociraptor teammate number 4, ready to make the final sprint to the finish.

Worse, Wesley was flagging now.

"Move!" yelled Daisy.

"Won't," he snapped back.

But Fergus could see from the sweat on his jersey and hear from his grunting that each turn of the pedals was proving harder and harder for Wesley.

"Will . . . not . . . lose," Wesley panted out. "Will . . . not . . . lose."

If you let me through the team will win, Fergus thought angrily. *You'd still be a winner.*

Thankfully, with just metres to go, someone else thought the very same thing.

"NOW!" yelled Daisy, and flicking hard right, she pulled out of Dermot's path and pushed the whimpering Wesley, who had no energy to fight her, out of the way too.

"Now!" Fergus roared to himself, and dug harder and deeper than he had ever dug before. It paid off, and that reserve of energy he'd saved, the same reserve Wesley had squandered, saw him fly forward and right past Lala Jones with only seconds to spare.

"You're going to make it!" he heard Jambo shout from the finish line. "Flying Fergus does it again!" Mum cheered.

"This is for the team!" Fergus yelled in his head. "All of you." And then he thought of someone else who had been with him the whole way, at least in his head: his dad. As he crossed the white line, the sound of cameras snapping and the crowd going wild, Fergus dinged his bell hard, again and again, sounding out his victory for the team, and for his friends in Nevermore.

The Best of Both Worlds

The first person to hug him was Daisy. Then came Grandpa, then Mum and Jambo, Chimp jumping beside them, then Minnie and Calamity, until Fergus felt like he was in the arms of an enormous and excited octopus.

"Nice one, Fergie," Calamity said, patting him on the back.

"Totally BEAST!" yelled Daisy.

"You did it!" Mum whispered proudly into his ear, her cheek against his wet with tears of happiness.

Fergus nodded, his "thanks" muffled against Jambo's shoulder, his own tears choked back because there was NO WAY he was crying, not in front of Daisy, or Wesley for that matter. Which reminded him . . .

He pulled himself out of the hug enough to get out the words: "*We* did it," he said. "It wasn't just me, it was all of us."

"*Most* of us," said Daisy, raising an eyebrow.

Fergus looked at Wesley and Dermot, who were sat sullenly on the ground next to them, with Choppy giving them a good talking-to. "No," he insisted. "*All* of us." And, to Daisy's and everyone's shock, he held out his hand to pull Wesley to his feet.

"You're one slick cyclist," he said.

Wesley nodded. "You're not so bad either," he conceded.

The corners of Fergus's mouth twitched. That, coming from Wesley, was the biggest compliment he had ever been given.

"Haven't you got something else to say?" Choppy nudged his son forward.

Wesley scowled. "Sorry," he mumbled, then turned to go. But Choppy nudged him again and he turned back, holding something out to Fergus in his hand. "This is yours," he said.

Fergus took it and smiled as he realized what it was: the Number One jersey. He knew he should be angry – he should be telling Wesley off for messing with the team tactics – but he couldn't feel any of that hot electricity in him right now, just happiness. "Thanks," he said.

Wesley shrugged. "Whatever."

"Whatever?" demanded Daisy. "WHATEVER?! We just won the Nationals, Wesley, or had you forgotten?"

Slowly, a smile spread across Wesley's face. "Och, we did!" he exclaimed, as if he was only realizing it for the first time. "We did!"

"Well, Hercules' Hopefuls did," said Daisy. "You're one of us now."

Wesley snorted. "Today, maybe. But you wait until next season: we'll be back as Wallace's Winners, fighting fit and beating you by miles."

"Yeah, we'll see," grinned Fergus.

"A pound says I'll have five seconds on you by next week," Wesley challenged.

Fergus went to shake on it, then remembered something. "Hang on," he said. "Back in a minute."

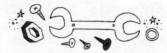

Grandpa was surrounded by reporters – probably talking nineteen to the dozen about how this had been his life's dream, Fergus thought to himself. Saying something totally embarrassing, no doubt.

"Here he is," Grandpa called when he saw Fergus pushing through the press pack. "My brilliant boy!"

Fergus felt his cheeks flush. "Och, all in a day's work," he joked.

"That's our Flying Fergie," Grandpa said. "As modest as he is magnificent."

Fergus reddened again.

"So are you looking forward to taking on the London Lions?" one reporter demanded, thrusting a microphone in his face.

"Your mum must be incredibly proud," said another. "Has she come to watch you today?"

"What about your dad?" asked a third. "What does he think about you taking on the world?"

Fergus felt a cold wave wash over him. "I – I don't . . . " he stammered before turning to Grandpa for help.

"That's enough," Grandpa said, putting his hand over the microphone. "He's exhausted, poor boy. But if you come to the shop this week, I'll be glad to answer your questions. Hercules' Hand-Me-Downs on Napier Street. Can't miss it."

And with that, he pulled Fergus out of the crowd. When they were far enough away from the reporters they sank down onto some empty seats, among discarded streamers and party poppers, Grandpa holding Fergus by the shoulders and looking at him, his face never more serious. "Your dad *would* be proud, you know that, don't you?" he said.

Fergus nodded.

"But you know that he's not coming back, don't you?"

Fergus swallowed hard. "I do," he said. And for the first time, it wasn't a lie.

"But that doesn't mean you haven't got everything you need," continued Grandpa. "Me and your mammy, we love you more than anything. And Chimp too, of course."

"I know," said Fergus, feeling a warm glow from Grandpa's words. "But . . ."

"But what?" Grandpa asked.

Fergus thought. He'd been about to blurt it all out. His secret life in a parallel universe. The way he'd rescued his dad from a mean king. The fact that he was going back for good to race in Nevermore. But was he? Today had been immense . . . Brilliotic . . . BEAST! How could he give that up forever? How could he let his team down? Or his enemies for that matter: Wesley had bet him a pound on a head to head.

"Nothing," Fergus said finally. "I was just wondering if you won your bet with Major Menzies?"

"Oh, that!" Grandpa grinned. "Not exactly. We upped it instead."

Fergus frowned. "What do you mean?"

"Double or quits," explained Grandpa. "A hundred pounds on you winning the Internationals next year."

Fergus laughed. "Well, in that case,

guess I'd better stick around."

"Thinking of going somewhere, were you?" asked Grandpa, still smiling.

Fergus shook his head. "Never," he said. "At least, not for too long, anyway."

As Fergus lay in bed that night every inch of his body was throbbing, yet somehow the aches felt strangely delicious, as if they were a badge of honour he'd earned by working so hard.

"What do you reckon then, Chimp?" he asked, leaning painfully over the side of the bed to peer at his dog who was chewing happily on a shoe.

Chimp cocked an interested ear at his friend.

"We stay here," Fergus explained. "Stay on the team. Just go back to Nevermore for visits. Maybe an extended summer holiday . . . " He paused as an idea popped into his head and took root. "A training camp!" he exclaimed. "I could work alongside Dad. Assistant coach, maybe. How does that sound?"

Chimp sighed as he settled back down to some serious chewing.

"Why am I asking you?" Fergus shook his head and smiled. "As if you can answer." And he switched off the light and settled down to sleep, ready to dream of crossing the finish line, a winner at the Nationals.

Chimp waited until he could hear the gentle sound of Fergus snoring before dropping the shoes and settling himself. "Ripping idea, mate," he whispered into the night. "Totally bonzer." He scratched half-heartedly at a flea on his flank. "Even if I do say so myself."

Joanna Nadin is the author of more than fifty books for children and teenagers, including the bestselling Rachel Riley Diaries and the award-winning Penny Dreadful series. Amongst other accolades she has been nominated for the Carnegie Medal and shortlisted for the Roald Dahl Funny Prize, and is the winner of the Fantastic Book Award, Highland Book Award and the Surrey Book Award. Joanna has been a journalist and adviser to the Prime Minister, and now teaches creative writing at Bath Spa University. She lives in Bath and loves to ride her rickety bicycle, but doesn't manage to go very fast. And she never, ever back-pedals . . .

Sir Chris Hoy MBE, won his first Olympic gold medal in Athens 2004. Four years later in Beijing he became the first Briton since 1908 to win three gold medals in a single Olympic Games. In 2012, Chris won two gold medals at his home Olympics in London, becoming Britain's most successful Olympian with six gold medals and one silver. Sir Chris also won eleven World titles and two Commonwealth Games gold medals. In December 2008, Chris was voted BBC Sports Personality of the Year, and he received a Knighthood in the 2009 New Year Honours List. Sir Chris retired as a professional competitive cyclist in early 2013; he still rides almost daily. He lives in Manchester with his wife and son.

To discover more about Fergus and his friends join them at

FLYING FERGUS
.com

There's loads to explore – learn more about Chris Hoy, watch videos and get tips and tricks for safe cycling and taking care of your bike. You can play games, solve puzzles and even get exclusive sneak peeks of new books in the series!

JOIN THE GANG!

Become a member of the fan club to keep up to date with Fergus, Daisy and Chimp and be a part of all their adventures. You'll have the chance to build your own Flying Fergus character and even choose your own bike to ride!